Paddington at the Fair

by Michael Bond
pictures by David McKee

G. P. Putnam's Sons
New York

One summer day the Browns went on an outing to a part of London called Hampstead, where there was a big fair.

Paddington had never been to a fair before and he was most excited.

Mr. Brown gave Jonathan, Judy and Paddington a pound each. "I should make the most of it," he said. "It only happens once a year."

First of all, Paddington had a turn at the
Coconut Shy. He hit the man in charge by
mistake.

"That isn't a very good start," said Mrs.
Brown.

"Perhaps you should stand on something,"
suggested Judy.

Paddington thought that was a very good idea, and after two more turns he had won a china bird for his bedroom wall and a picture of a goldfish.

"I shall call the goldfish Hampstead," he said. "After the fair."

And he gave his prizes to Mrs. Bird to hold so that he would leave his paws free for the Merry-Go-Round.

Paddington liked the Merry-Go-Round so much he went on it a second time.

"I think it's a very good way of traveling if you don't want to go anywhere," he called as he went past. "Especially if you have plenty of marmalade sandwiches to keep you going."

While he was on the Merry-Go-Round
Paddington noticed the Helter-Skelter and
he was soon on his way up with a mat.

"Did you enjoy that?" asked Mr. Brown.

"Yes, thank you very much," said Paddington. "But it was a very quick way of spending ten pence."

"That's funny," said Mrs. Brown. "None of the other children are coming down. They all seem to be stuck."

"Oh, dear," said Paddington. "I think they may be sitting on one of my marmalade sandwiches."

"Perhaps we'd better go on the Space Craft before they find out," said Jonathan hastily.

Paddington liked anything new and he quickly climbed into an empty car.

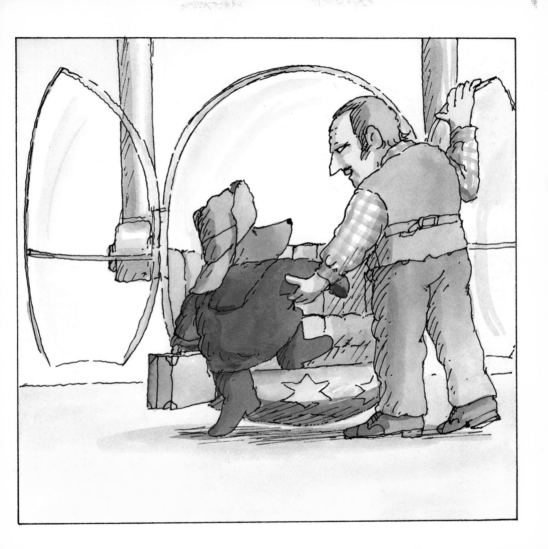

He soon wished he hadn't. One moment they were climbing slowly up toward the sky. The next moment they came shooting back down again at breakneck speed.

The cars went up and down and around and around. There were times when it felt as if they were going upside down as well.

"I wish I had chosen a different car," he groaned as they climbed out. "Mine felt as if it was trying to throw me out."

"I think they all felt the same," said Judy.

"Perhaps you should ask for your money back," joked Mr. Brown, as he helped Paddington to his feet.

"I may ask for my stomach back," said Paddington darkly.

"How about trying something a bit quieter for a change?" said Mrs. Brown.

"I don't think you'll find those very quiet!" called Jonathan.

But he was too late. Paddington was already climbing into a Dodgem car.

He soon found out why some people call them "Bumper cars."

By the time Paddington came off the
Dodgem cars it was getting late and he had
spent nearly all his money.

Just then he saw a tent with a notice
outside which said: MADAME GRANT –
FORTUNES TOLD.

"Perhaps she will tell me where my next
ten pence is coming from," he said, and
before the Browns could stop him he had
gone inside.

Madame Grant looked at Paddington, then she looked into her crystal ball. Then she looked at Paddington again.

It was very hot inside the tent and Paddington had his eyes closed.

"I think," she said, "I see a bear who is going to sleep very well tonight."

And she was quite right. Paddington slept
very well that night. In fact he slept so well
he didn't fall out of bed once; not even when
he dreamed he was back on the Space Craft.

Quality Printing and Binding by
Dai Pirp n Printing Co. (H-K.) Ltd
Tsuen Wan Industrial Centre
2/F-5, F 2 0-248, Texaco Road
Tsuen Wan, N.T.
Kowloon, Hong Kong